BLUE CHICKEN

Deborah Freedman

VIKING

An Imprint of Penguin Group (USA) Inc.

VIKING
Published by Penguin Group
Penguin Young Readers Group, 345 Hudson Street, New York, New York 10014, U.S.A.
Penguin Group (Canada), 90 Eglinton Avenue East, Suite 700, Toronto, Ontario, Canada M4P 2Y3
(a division of Pearson Penguin Canada Inc.)
Penguin Books Ltd, 80 Strand, London WC2R 0RL, England
Penguin Ireland, 25 St Stephen's Green, Dublin 2, Ireland (a division of Penguin Books Ltd)
Penguin Group (Australia), 250 Camberwell Road, Camberwell, Victoria 3124, Australia
(a division of Pearson Australia Group Pty Ltd)
Penguin Books India Pvt Ltd, 11 Community Centre, Panchsheel Park, New Delhi – 110 017, India
Penguin Group (NZ), 67 Apollo Drive, Rosedale, North Shore 0632, New Zealand
(a division of Pearson New Zealand Ltd.)
Penguin Books (South Africa) (Pty) Ltd, 24 Sturdee Avenue, Rosebank, Johannesburg 2196, South Africa

Penguin Books Ltd, Registered Offices: 80 Strand, London WC2R 0RL, England

First published in 2011 by Viking, a division of Penguin Young Readers Group

1 2 3 4 5 6 7 8 9 10

Copyright © Deborah Freeman, 2011
All rights reserved

LIBRARY OF CONGRESS CATALOGING-IN-PUBLICATION DATA IS AVAILABLE
ISBN: 978-0-670-01293-0
Manufactured in China   Set in Sabon   Book design by Jim Hoover

For my parents,
Joel and Naomi
Freedman

At last!

This picture is almost finished. The chickens are white, their coop is brown . . . and this day is perfect for painting the barn.

But wait. Does one of
the chickens want to help?

Instead of the barn,
she's painting herself!

She's toppled the BLUE.

And the spilled blue is spreading.
Till the ground grows blue, too!

Once-purple pansies
now bloom blue.

Blue-yellow ducklings
splatter the cat.

A moo wakes the chickens.
They're peevish and blue. They dump
the red wheelbarrow, dropping that
chicken who just wanted to . . .

HELP!

But the chicken is sorry!

Sincerely sorry.

Maybe the chicken
can undo the blue?

Maybe,

maybe,

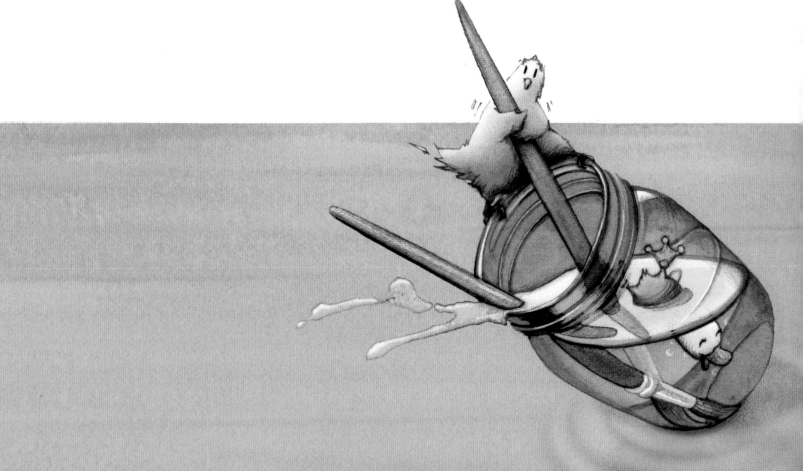

just maybe . . .

Look!

No. More. BLUE!

Except for the sky.

The sky should stay blue
on a morning so clear,

on a day that is perfect . . .

for painting the barn.